# Claudia the Pig Saves the Farm

Written by

Lisa Birnbaum

Illustrated by

Kit Turner

*For Kyle - for making my dream come true.*

Claudia the pig was born
on a warm sunny day,

on a farm in New Jersey
on the 2nd of May.

She had lots of brothers and sisters
with important pig names,

who spent their days
rolling in the mud
and playing piglet games.

But Claudia was different,
she was tiny as could be.
No bigger than a button,
tiny as a pea.

Although she was small,
her heart was so big.

Her Mama knew one day
she'd be a very important pig.

Her brothers and sisters said she was too little to play.
They said all she did was get in the way.

This made Claudia sad.
Being different was not easy.

She then met a ladybug who flew in light and breezy.

The ladybug's name was Ella
and they played all day,
jumping and running Claudia's sadness away.

But the best moment came
when she heard Ella say
that she too was born
on the 2nd of May.

The horse and cow,
the dog and cat too,
all helped the kind farmer
with special jobs he had to do.

Claudia wanted to help,
but how could she?

No bigger than a button, tiny as a pea.

Ella took her to meet her wise friend Rose.
She was the queen bee,
with a stinger on the tip of her nose.

She taught them the importance of the ants, the bees,
the fireflies, the spiders, the beetles,
and even the fleas.

The farm could not run without them
all working in kind,
even though the animals
paid these insects no mind.

Claudia asked Rose what her job was to be.
Rose said, "be patient and soon you will see!"

The animals loved the farmer.
He was kind to them all.

One day while working in the field,
he tripped and took a terrible fall.

The doctor was called in
and sent him straight to bed.

"You must stay there
for two weeks,"
the Doctor said.

The next morning the farmer's house
was filled with smoke.

"Help, help," cried the farmer
as he began to choke.

Claudia woke up to the kind farmer's cries.
She wiggled through the fence
because of her size.

She was so tiny she fit right through.
All the other animals were locked in
and didn't know what to do.

I will save the kind farmer,
don't worry about a thing.

"How can YOU save the farmer?"
they all began to sing.

Then Claudia said, "I may be little,
but I am mighty inside."

Then up to the gate Kate the horse did stride.
She said, "Go little pig, save the day somehow!"
"Be brave little pig," shouted Evelyn the cow.

They all wished her well, even Arya the cat,
who was still curled up on the barn floor mat.

Claudia knew just what she had to do.
She went to get Ella and queen bee Rose too.

They gathered together all the ants and the bees,
the fireflies, spiders, beetles and fleas.

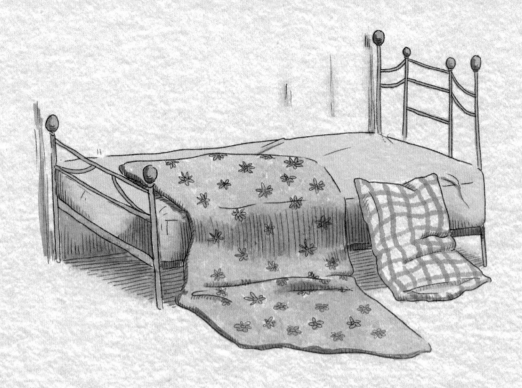

When they got to the farmer,
Claudia was the one to speak.

"I have come to save you, kind farmer,
but alone I would be too weak.

With all these tiny friends by my side,
we will pick you up and get you outside."

They pushed and they pulled
and they tugged with all their might.

And to the surprise of the kind farmer,
Claudia was right!

The kind farmer thanked Claudia
and all her tiny friends.

Then Claudia looked at the house
and saw smoke coming from both ends.

She hopped on the back
of queen bee Rose.

They flew to the barn
and grabbed the hose.

With the help of all her tiny friends,
she saved the day!

The fire was out,
and the farmer got away.

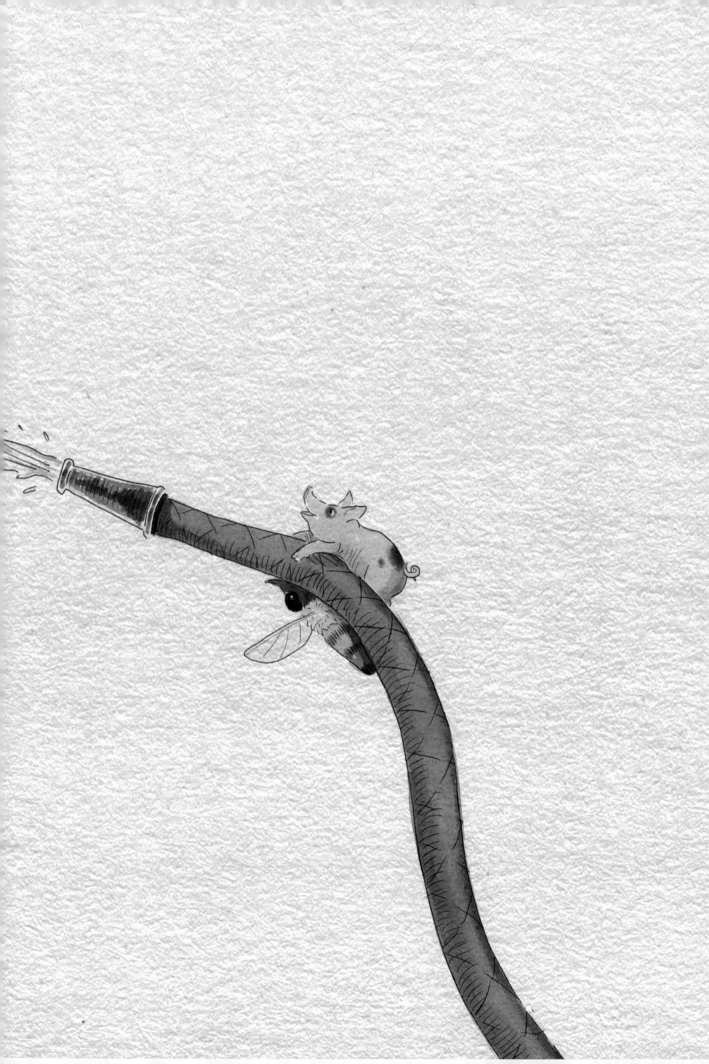

That night there was a party as big as could be
for this tiny little pig, no bigger than a pea.

Everyone was there, all her old friends and new,
the horse and the cow, and Arya the cat too.

Rose brought all the ants, the bees,
fireflies, spiders, beetles and fleas.

The animals promised that from now on
they would work together,
and they would all be friends
forever and ever.

Claudia was so happy
with her best friend Ella by her side
and queen bee Rose watching over them,
bursting with pride.

But the best part of the day
was when they remembered

it was the 2nd of May.

"Happy Birthday," they all shouted.
"Hip hip hooray!"

To this tiny pig hero,
who just saved the day.

The following year
a new litter of piglets came to be.

Emma, Connor, Ava,
Reese, Noah and Callie.

Each one had a special gift
it was plain to see.

With all of their powers
they made a perfect superhero team.

But someone was missing
that would make them supreme.

Then one day they
heard a little squeal,

in the corner of the barn
by the old wagon wheel.

Out popped Teddy
prefect as could be,

no bigger than a button,
tiny as a pea!

Claudia will teach them to be brave.
She will teach them to be kind.

Now let's see what new adventures
these little piglets will find...

Made in the USA
Las Vegas, NV
08 December 2023

82296436R00021